D0229765

Moonthief

For Tom and Caroline – RMcG
For Marcia with love – PD

KINGFISHER
An imprint of Kingfisher Publications Plc
New Penderel House, 283-288 High Holborn, London WC1V 7HZ
www.kingfisherpub.com

First published by Kingfisher 2002
10 9 8 7 6 5 4 3 2 1

Text copyright © Roger McGough 2002
Illustrations copyright © Penny Dann 2002

The moral right of the author and illustrator has been asserted.
All rights reserved. No part of this publication may be reproduced, stored in a retrieval
system or transmitted by any means, electronic, mechanical, photocopying or otherwise,
without the prior permission of the publisher.

A CIP catalogue record for this book is available from the British Library.

ISBN 0 7534 0662 4

Printed in Singapore
1TR/TWP/CG(CG)/170NYA

Moonthief

Roger McGough

Illustrated by Penny Dann

KING*f*ISHER

**LONDON BOROUGH OF SUTTON
LIBRARY SERVICE**

02281232 7	
Askews	Feb-2004
JF	

"Look, there's a new moon out tonight," said Bobby.

"I wonder what they did with the old one," said Betty.

½ full honey

½ empty honey

Runny Honey

HONEY FOR PIES

FIZZY HONEY

STILL HONEY

UPSIDE-DOWN HONEY

"It's on the shelf in my honey-cupboard, wrapped in silver paper and tied with pink ribbons," said Bobby.

Onion Honey

FUNNY HONEY

SUNNY HONEY

"But how did it get there?"

"I stole it."

"Moon

"I hitched a ride

on a shooting

star and while

the man-in-the-

moon had his

back turned, I

blew it up with

a bicycle pump

and floated back

down to earth."

"Phew!" said Betty, her eyes
wide open. "But why?"
"To give to you."
She smiled mischievously.
"Silly Bear, what could I
do with an old moon?"

"You could take it
to bed with you,"
said Bobby.

"Instead of
my teddy?"

"You could train it
to fetch your slippers."

"You can't teach
an old moon
new tricks."

"You could keep
goldfish in it . . ."

"GOLDFISH!"

"Or, you could play frisbee with it," said Bobby.

"If it went spinning into the sky . . .

it might never come back," said Betty.

"You could lead the big parade with it," said Bobby. "Dumpity, Dumpity, Dum. Dumpity, Dumpity–"

"It wouldn't be fair to beat the moon,"
said Betty.
"Dum!" said Bobby, and then thought
for a while.

the Big Parade

"You could use it as a silver tray
and serve chilled drinks upon it."
"Mmm . . ." mmmed Betty.

BETTYWOOD

"Lay it down on the lawn
and lounge beside it."

"Or, you could hang it up in the bathroom when you're fixing your hair with the pink ribbons I just knew would come in useful."

Bear Spray

Betty reflected on the idea.

"You could
hang it from the
highest branches of
our favourite tree so
that we could have
moonlight all day
and every day . . ."

"Or," said Bobby, becoming really
excited now . . .

"You could score goals with it

play tenpin bowls with it

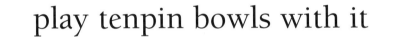

go ice-skating on it

trampolining on it . . .

or . . .
or . . .
or . . .

you could be the first
lady bear on the moon!"

BEAR SPORT

BETTY SCORES
WINNING GOAL!

BEAR TIMES

BETTY is FIRST
SEE PAGES 1, 2, 4, 5, 8,
and 10

SPACE HERO!

Betty interrupted.
"But what about the man?"

"What man?"

"The man-in-the-moon, silly. Does he know you've stolen it?"

"I didn't actually *steal* it," said Bobby. "I just borrowed it for a few hours."

Betty looked at him sternly. "I think you should put it back where it belongs, don't you?"

"I suppose so," said Bobby, shrugging his shoulders.

Then, taking off his glasses
and polishing them with a
dock leaf, he said quietly,
"I just wanted to give you
the most brilliant present
in the whole universe."

"Oh, you Silly Bear," said Betty, and taking hold of his paw gave it a big squeeze.

I don't want the moon, or the sun, or the stars, because . . .

of all the bears
in this wide, wide,
moonlit world . . ."

Bobby began to blush . . .

and blush, and blush, and blush, and blush . . .

"All I want is . . .

you."